HOCKEY RULES!

Irene Punt

illustrations by
Ken Steacy

Scholastic Canada Ltd.
Toronto New York London Auckland Sydney
Mexico City New Delhi Hong Kong Buenos Aires

Scholastic Canada Ltd.
604 King Street West, Toronto, Ontario M5V 1E1, Canada

Scholastic Inc.
557 Broadway, New York, NY 10012, USA

Scholastic Australia Pty Limited
PO Box 579, Gosford, NSW 2250, Australia

Scholastic New Zealand Limited
Private Bag 94407, Botany, Manukau 2163, New Zealand

Scholastic Children's Books
Euston House, 24 Eversholt Street, London NW1 1DB, UK

www.scholastic.ca

Library and Archives Canada Cataloguing in Publication
Punt, Irene, 1955-
Hockey rules! / Irene Punt ; illustrations by Ken Steacy.

ISBN 978-0-545-99765-2

I. Steacy, Ken II. Title.
PS8581.U56H62 2008   jC813'.54   C2008-901888-5

ISBN-10 0-545-99765-8

Text copyright © 2008 by Irene Punt.
Illustrations copyright © 2008 by Scholastic Canada Ltd.
All rights reserved.

8 7 6   Printed in Canada 121   14 15 16

MIX
Paper from
responsible sources
FSC® C004071

Contents

To Harty — for your love of the game,
as a player and a ref

— I.P.

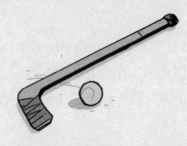

Road Hockey

Tom ran with the road hockey ball, stickhandling it toward the sidewalk. With a quick flick, he took a shot. Jordan caught it in his goalie glove.

"Sweet save!" said Jeff, flashing his crooked smile. Jeff was Tom's babysitter. He'd played hockey for ten years and knew everything about it.

Jordan gloated. "Na, na! No goals on me!" He tossed the ball onto the street. It rolled right to Stuart. Stuart slapped his stick and the ball dribbled into the net.

"Woo hoo! Great goal!" cheered Jeff, with a high-five.

Jordan made his scary goalie face and everyone laughed.

"Okay, road rats, time to shut the game down for tonight," said Jeff.

"What?" protested Tom. "Not yet!"

Jeff held up his hand. "'Fraid so. All of us have homework, right?"

"Homework? Yuck!" said Mark. "Road hockey is my kind of homework. It's practice for our next hockey game."

Tom, Mark, Stuart and Jordan played hockey for the Glenlake Hawks and they were supposed to practise as much as possible. "Yeah, Coach Howie's orders! Hockey homework," said Tom.

Jeff laughed. "Okay, okay. But only five more minutes." He unleashed a wrist shot.

Tom and his friends ran after the ball, cheering, "Hockey rules! Yay, Jeff! Jeff's the best!"

At 7:15 Jordan's watch beeped.

At 7:16 Stuart's mom phoned. "Get home!"

At 7:17 Mark's sister came by. "Home. Now!"

The game was officially over. Jordan shouldered his goalie pads. "Hey, Jeff, I want you to be my babysitter!" he said.

"Me, too!" said Stuart. "Pleeeeease!"

Jeff answered, "Sorry, Tom's mom has me totally booked up. Plus, I also . . ."

"Lucky Tom!" chimed his friends.

Yeah, thought Tom. *Jeff is the best and he's all mine.*

Rules Are Rules

The next night. Six o'clock. Centennial Arena.

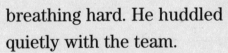

Coach Howie blew his whistle and motioned everyone in. Tom skated over, breathing hard. He huddled quietly with the team.

"Hawks, great drills tonight. You guys have been working hard and it's paying off!" said Coach Howie, clapping. "The Hockey Calgary website says we are rated number . . . ONE!"

"We're number one! We're number one!"

Everyone cheered, banging their sticks on the ice. Tom liked Coach Howie. He liked his team. It felt great to be the best.

"Any questions tonight?" asked Coach Howie.

Tom wanted to ask about offside. Like lots of his teammates, he still didn't understand the rule about waiting for the puck to cross the blue line first.

"I've got a question," said Mark. "Should I get a hot dog or pickle chips after practice?"

Tom elbowed him.

Coach Howie rolled his eyes and cleared his throat. "Okay, then. Let's scrimmage for the last fifteen minutes. Split into two groups. Dark jerseys against light jerseys. Five on the ice, two on the bench."

Stuart, a defenceman, and Jordan, a goalie, wore dark jerseys. Tom waved for Mark to stand with him. They both wore white jerseys.

The teams were ready. Coach Howie stood at centre ice. He dropped the puck. Tom won the faceoff, followed by a perfect pass to Mark.

Mark grabbed the puck and headed down the ice. Stuart followed, swiping at the puck. Mark lifted his stick for a slapshot. *WHUMPT!* It came down on Stuart's shoulder. Stuart lay on the ice like a starfish.

"Oooww-aaah," he groaned.

Coach Howie blew his whistle and the game stopped. He crouched down beside Stuart. "You okay?"

Stuart's eyes were blank. "Yup." He stood slowly, with Mark's help. "Ooowwwhh . . ."

The team clapped their sticks on the ice.

Coach Howie's voice was firm. "Listen up. That was a high stick. You can't let this happen. You've got to control your stick! You could hit someone on the head. Give him a concussion. And it's a two-minute penalty — five minutes if there's an injury. Rules are rules."

Mark frowned. "I was only trying to score."

Coach Howie looked serious. "Everyone, watch this." He began to lift his stick. "Say stop when it's too high."

Up went his stick.

"STOP!" almost everyone yelled at the

same time, because almost everyone knew the high-sticking spot — above an opponent's shoulder.

"Okay, good! Now, NO high sticks!" Coach Howie dropped the puck for a faceoff.

A few minutes later, he stopped the game and reviewed the tripping penalty as Stuart rubbed his shins.

Tom rested on the bench with Mark.

"Remember when Coach Howie was more fun? He used to let us scrimmage without all these interruptions." Mark let out a giant breath. "Now it's start and stop and start and stop. We're just trying to score goals, right?"

Tom glanced at Coach Howie, about to blow his whistle again. "Hockey players who get lots of penalties are goons. I don't want to be a goon. Do you?"

Mark laughed. "Older players are goons, not us. They wipe players out on purpose. We're just trying to win. And to stay number one!" He rubbed his stomach. "I'm so hungry, I could eat ten hot dogs and ten bags of pickle chips."

Suddenly, two white-jersey players flew to the bench. Tom and Mark quickly scrambled onto the ice into position. The puck slammed into Mark's stick. He passed the puck to Tom. Tom stickhandled it along the boards and behind the net. With a smooth turn, he did a perfect wraparound shot, and the puck slid by Jordan's goalie skate.

Coach Howie pointed at the net and smiled.

"Goal!" cheered Tom. "Yes!" He pumped the air with his fist. "Yahoo!"

BANG! BANG! BANG! Tom looked around. He could hear someone banging on the spectator glass and shouting full volume, "Yay, Tom! Great goal! You RULE!"

Jeff the Ref

At 6:15 the buzzer sounded. Practice was over.

Tom, Stuart, Mark and Jordan skated across the ice. When they got to the open gate, Jeff was waiting with a bag of chocolate caramels.

"Jeff!" yelped the boys, huddling around him.

"Great goal!" exclaimed Jeff. "Nice assist!" He slapped Tom and Mark high-fives.

Tom reached for a handful of candy. "Hey, what are you doing here?"

Jeff waved a small book. It was the same one he had been studying the other night —

Hockey Canada: Official Playing Rules. There was a picture of a referee on the front cover. "I just passed the test. Now I'm a ref!"

"All right!" The boys whooped.

Jeff leaned toward them and whispered, "I'm a little nervous about being a ref, so you guys need to cheer me on."

They began to chant. "Jeff the Ref! Jeff the Ref! Jeff is the best!"

Jeff smiled. "Thanks, guys."

The four boys made their way to the dressing room, chanting faster and faster, "Jeff the Ref! Jeff the Ref! Jeff is the best!"

Tom swung open the door and announced to everyone, "My sitter is going to be the best ref in the world!"

"Yaaaaay, JEFF!" Mark screamed so loud, his mouthguard fell out.

Jordan looked at Tom enviously. "You're so lucky to have Jeff for your babysitter."

Tom smiled a lumpy chocolate caramel smile. He couldn't agree more.

City Helpers

Thursday. At school.

Tom, Mark, Stuart and Jordan sat at an art table drawing pictures of themselves for Social Studies as Mrs. Wong, their teacher, decorated a new bulletin board.

Stuart coloured a black eye on his picture. He was accident-prone and always had at least one bruise.

Jordan drew his scary goalie face.

"Here I am, wearing my Flames jersey," said Tom. "It used to be Jeff's."

"I'm going to give myself a moustache!" said Mark, looking for the brown marker.

Tom laughed. Mark always cracked him up.

"No way!" said Kylie, standing behind them. "Your portrait is supposed to be authentic. Like, *real*. Stop fooling around." She scooped up a handful of markers and went back to her table.

"Hey!" said Stuart. "Now there's no dark red marker for scabs. And no beige for Band-Aids. How am I supposed to finish my picture?"

"Bring those markers back!" growled Jordan.

Kylie made a face.

"She should draw devil horns on hers," joked Mark.

Snop. Snop. Snop. Mrs. Wong stapled a map of Calgary onto the bulletin board. *Snop. Snop. Snop.* She stapled paper question marks around the map.

"Okay, people," said Mrs. Wong. "When your portrait is cut out, staple it to the 'Our City' bulletin board. And now — I'd like you

16

to think about our city and all the people who help to make it work. Who are our city helpers?"

Like an explosion, half the class called out answers at the same time. "Firefighter!" "Police officer!" "Letter carrier!" "Baker!" "Doctor!" "Nurse!" "Hairdresser!" "Bus driver!"

"Excellent! Choose one that you'd like to know more about and draw that person.

Their pictures will go on our bulletin board, too. Because . . . we are going to invite them to our classroom!" Mrs. Wong waved her hands in the air. "And even more exciting . . ."

She opened the cupboard behind her desk. Eight Monopoly games were stacked on the middle shelf. "You will get to play Monopoly with our visitors — and ask them questions about our city."

"Yay!" everyone cheered.

Monopoly! Tom's eyes lit up. He loved Monopoly. He always played it with Grandma Dot. And he always won.

Amber Woznicki waved her hand. "You all know my dad, Officer Woz. He could be a visitor. And he's the best Monopoly player in the police department. I'm going to draw a picture of him in his police uniform."

"Hey, Tom," said Mark. "Wait till Officer Woz plays Monopoly with *you*! We'll see who's the best."

Tom said, "Right on!" He could see himself owning hotels and houses on Boardwalk.

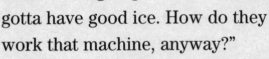

"I'm drawing a Zamboni driver," said Mark to his group. "You gotta have good ice. How do they work that machine, anyway?"

"I'm drawing the Flames goalie," said Jordan.

"I can draw Coach Howie," said Stuart. "With the water bottles."

"Hockey, hockey, hockey," said Kylie with a groan. "How does *hockey* help our city?"

"Guess who I'm going to draw?" asked Tom. He tried to come up with somebody good. Fast.

"Who?" Kylie asked.

"A babysitter! Some parents can't work if they don't have one!" Tom flashed a toothy smile. He reached for a black marker and began to draw Jeff, wearing a black-and-white striped referee jersey.

"Good thinking!" Mrs. Wong nodded at Tom. "All people who work hard help to make our city better. It's a *team* effort." She held up some lined paper. "Your assignment, everyone, is to write down some amazing questions for our city helpers. Your good copies will go up on the board next to your pictures."

She wrote on the blackboard:

OUR CITY Homework — by Monday!

1. Finish your good copy of questions.

2. Read the Monopoly rules.

"Knowing the rules is important," said Mrs. Wong. "Playing by the rules makes the game fair for everyone. And I want lots of questions!"

Tom grinned. "Here's one: When's our next hockey game at Calgary Centennial Arena? And the answer is — Saturday. Two o'clock."

He and his friends all stuck two thumbs up.

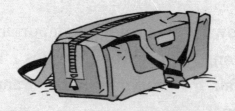

Game Time

Saturday. One o'clock.

"Everyone in the car!" hollered Dad.

"Okay," said Mom. She rushed around the house, turning off lights and grabbing her jacket, gloves and a blanket.

Tom and Mark loaded their hockey bags and sticks into the trunk.

"Are you sure you've got everything?" asked Mom.

"Yup." Tom nodded. "But we need to pick up Jordan."

They pulled up in front of Jordan's house. Mom honked. Several minutes later, Jordan stumbled out the door, lugging his huge

goalie bag. Tom wished he had the courage to tell him to stop being late.

Jordan stuffed his bag and stick into the trunk. "Homework," he growled. "My mom made me start on those questions! I hate writing." He lowered his voice. "So far, I just used Kylie's: How does hockey help our city?"

"Did I hear homework?" asked Mom.

"We have to write questions about our city," said Tom.

"Like . . .?" asked Mom.

"Who delivers mail to the Calgary Flames?" joked Mark.

"A firefighter!" chuckled Dad.

"Wow, you got it! Flames!"

Everyone laughed.

"Here's another question. What team do we play?" asked Mark.

"Brentwood Bears," said Jordan.

"Oh, no, Brentwood Bears! Those guys are BIG!" said Tom. "They've got that giant guy on defence! He wears *men's* shoulder pads and he's way taller than me."

"They freak me out," said Mark.

"The Bears should be going after the puck, not the players," said Mom.

"Maybe Jeff will be your ref!" added Dad.

"Yeah!" said Tom. "Jeff the Ref. Jeff is the best! He'll protect us!"

"Well — a ref is there to protect the *rules*," said Mom.

The boys rolled their eyes.

The car finally turned off busy Crowchild Trail and headed toward the arena. Tom looked at the clock on the dashboard. His stomach twisted. "Step on the gas, Mom. We're going to be late!"

She slowed down.

"Mom! Pleeeeease go faster!"

"Sorry, guys." Mom pointed to the playground. "I'll get a speeding ticket."

Tom scrunched his forehead. "Here's a question for Officer Woz: Why do we have to go slow here when it makes us late for hockey?"

Jeff Is the Best

They hurried through the arena doors and down the hall to their dressing room. Everyone inside was ready for the game.

"Where were you guys?" asked Stuart.

"I was getting worried," said Coach Howie. "Remember — the rule is to be here half an hour before game time."

Tom hated being late. He watched the rest of his team file out the door.

Mark didn't look up. He was searching through his bag for something.

—————●—————

Both teams were into their warm-ups.

The Hawks skated fast backward, in a tight circle. Tom launched onto the ice. He kept his eyes down as he broke into the line of skaters. When he lifted his head, he saw — Jeff!

Jeff was wearing black pants, a black-and-white striped referee jersey and a special helmet with a clear visor. He had a shiny whistle wrapped around his knuckles and his ref's rule book poked out of his back pocket.

"Hey, Jeff!" called Tom.

Jeff looked over and gave him a weird half wave.

"Where's the linesman?" Tom asked Coach Howie.

"We just have one ref today," he said. "He'll be busy."

BUZZZZZ. The time clock sounded.

The team huddled around Jordan. They yelled "HAWKS!" and then took their positions.

Jeff stood at centre ice. Tom tried to stay cool, but excitement bubbled inside. *Jeff the Ref! Jeff the Ref! Jeff is the BEST!* He had always wished he could play on the same team as Jeff. This was the next best thing.

Jeff leaned forward. He blew his whistle. With a shaky *plop* the puck dropped. Not the best. It bounced — then rolled like a doughnut on the loose.

Tom flicked his stick and the puck went

right to the Bears' centre. The Bear flew down the ice. Jeff followed, his eyes glued to the action.

Tom dug in his blades and bolted after the puck. He reached out his stick.

THWACK! Tom felt his legs disappear. He hit the ice.

Jeff's hand went up. His whistle blew. He signalled tripping on the Bear who nailed Tom.

Tom shook himself as he stood. Wincing, he rubbed his wrist. "Oooooh," he moaned softly. He heard Jeff make the call at the scorekeeper's window: "Number 16 Bears — two minutes for tripping."

For a second Tom's wince became a smile. Jeff was an awesome ref. Probably the best ref ever — if you didn't count the puck drop.

— • —

The Hawks were now on a power play with only four Bears on the ice. Tom stood in the players' box. His wrist throbbed.

"These guys are huge!" said Stuart.

Tom tried not to think about the size of the Bears. When he'd faced off with their giant centre, he had tried not to look at him. *Stay brave*, Tom told himself. *We're the best! We RULE!* He looked at Mark. "This is our big chance to score. We're five on four." They got ready to step onto the ice.

"Keep your heads up," said Coach Howie.
Tom rushed into the action.

The Bears didn't let up. They skated in front of the Hawks net, trying to block Jordan's view. Jordan went into a crouch. A Bear blasted a backhand wrist shot. Jordan deflected the puck. Another Bear took a shot.

WHOMP! The puck slid through Jordan's legs and into the net.

Tom's heart sank. How did the Bears score short-handed?

WHEEEEE! Jeff blew his whistle. But he did not point at the net. He crossed his arms in front of his chest, then swept them outward.

"What . . . ?" Tom nudged Mark.

"No goal!" announced Jeff. "Net was off!"

"Ohhhhhhhhh!" wailed the players on the Bears bench. They shook their sticks and stomped their skates. Wearing black jerseys

and helmets, they looked like angry, *real* black bears.

"Woo HOO!" cheered the Hawks, as Jeff set their net in proper position.

Coach Howie said, "Keep the cheering down. A ref can give us a bench penalty."

"Not Jeff!" said Tom. "He's our friend."

Coach Howie's face went red. "Right now, Tom, Jeff is the ref first and your friend second."

Hawks vs. Bears

Second period. The score was 0–0.

"Go, Hawks, go!" cheered the spectators from the stands.

But no matter how hard and fast they played, the Hawks couldn't score.

"Keep trying," said Coach Howie. "Go full out."

Tom tried to think about shooting and scoring — and skating fast. The problem was, the fast skating was making him tired. And the Bears seemed to be getting bigger and stronger — and faster!

It was now the third period. The score was still 0–0. "Go, Hawks, go!" yelled the Hawks bench. The puck flew end to end. Up and down the ice it passed, from one player to the next.

Finally Tom had the puck. The biggest Bear defenceman charged forward. Tom deked around him. *BAM!* The Bear knocked Jeff over and fell on top of him, sending them spinning round and round. *WHEEEE!* Jeff blew his whistle and at the same instant, Tom unleashed his wicked slapshot. *Ping!* The puck flew right into the net.

"Goal!" exclaimed Tom. A rush of excitement bolted through him. "Yes! Yes! Yes!" He pumped the air with his fist.

"Yahoo!" cheered the Hawks.

"YAY!" cheered the fans.

But Jeff signalled no goal.

"No goal?" gasped the Hawks.

Jeff skated over, brushing the frost off his pants. "I lost sight of the puck when the Bears player fell on top of me," he explained. "I had to blow the whistle."

"That was a beautiful goal," said Stuart, punching Tom's shoulder. "I saw it." Tom skated toward the bench, deflated. *How in the world could Jeff miss my wicked slapshot — and the goal?*

———●———

The clock was running out of time.

"Let's go, Hawks, let's go!" hollered the fans.

Mark had the puck. He skated neck and neck with a Bear toward the blue line. As he raised his stick to pass — *WHAM!* The Bear fell.

Jeff's whistle blew.

Again? thought Tom. Then he saw Jeff's call.

"High stick." Jeff pointed to Mark. "And — offside!" Jeff pointed to Tom.

Tom checked his feet. He was on the wrong side of the blue line. *This is so unfair! It's like the Hawks can't do anything right.*

Jeff skated Mark over to the penalty box.

"I was only trying to pass," said Mark.

Jeff stopped. He looked at Mark. "Where's your mouthguard?" he asked. "Once your penalty's up, you can't go back on the ice without one."

"Huh?" said Mark. "But I couldn't find it!"

"I think it fell out when you cheered for Jeff at practice," said Stuart.

"You're off the ice as of right now," said Jeff. "Minor Hockey rule."

Mark plopped down on the bench. "Guys, can I borrow a mouthguard?"

"YUCK!" everyone screamed.

Jeff skated into position and dropped the puck at the faceoff dot.

The Bears won the faceoff and began charging down the ice. Then Stuart, skating backwards, tripped over his feet, leaving the Bears with a three-on-one.

"Oh, no!" gasped Tom. He tried to catch up to the rush.

Tic-tac-toe. *SWOOSH!* The puck sat in the back of the net, following the Bears' perfect passing play and goal.

"YAY!" screamed the Bears, banging their sticks.

Jordan dug out the puck. Tom couldn't believe his eyes.

Jeff Is the Worst

The final score was 1–0 — for the Bears.

As Tom filed into line to shake hands, he saw Jeff skate slowly off the ice. Anger burned inside him. *Why had Jeff been so mean to the Hawks?*

Comments swirled around Tom as the team headed for the dressing room.

"Your goal should have counted."

"We were robbed — big time."

"Jeff was the *worst!*"

"He called everything! Even two at a time! That's . . ."

"Unreal!"

"Unbelievable!"

In the noisy dressing room Tom sat holding a small bag of ice on his throbbing wrist. He peeked under the bag. His skin was turning blue.

Coach Howie blew his whistle. "We've got a lot of work to do next practice." He waved the game sheet in the air, and pointed to the list of penalties. "We played short-handed for eight minutes due to penalties. We made mistakes. And it killed us. We are better than that. Remember what I said at the last practice: use skills, not tricks. Do your best. And wear your mouthguard." He looked directly at Mark, then at Tom and Jordan, too. "And — don't be late!"

Everyone took a deep breath. They all

knew the Hawks were better than that. And it didn't feel good to be reminded.

Coach Howie walked over to Tom. "How's the wrist?"

Tom's eyes were wet. "Okay," he answered. But he could feel it swelling up like a jumbo sausage.

"Good," said Coach Howie. "That was a bad trip you got from that Bear. You're lucky it's not broken." He sighed. "I hate to see any player hurt. Doesn't matter what team they're on. That's what ended all my hopes of playing for the NHL. I got smashed into the boards and wrecked my knee. Nobody in the NHL wants a hockey player with a bad knee. Or a bad wrist."

Tom gulped. *He always dreamed of playing for the NHL!*

Jordan looked at Tom. "That Bear should have gotten five minutes for hurting you. And he should've been kicked out!"

"Here, this fell out of Jeff's pocket," Coach Howie said. He passed Tom Jeff's book, *Hockey Canada: Official Playing Rules*. "Please give it to him the next time you see him."

Tom shoved the book to the bottom of his bag — next to his smelly socks.

Dead Ducks

Sunday.

Knock, knock, knock. When Tom opened his front door, Jordan, Mark and Stuart were there, ready to play road hockey.

"Homework first!" hollered Mom from the kitchen. "Have you written up those questions? And gone over the Monopoly rules?"

Mark frowned. "I've got a new question: Why did Jeff call high sticking on me? I was just trying to pass the puck. And that Bears guy was way bigger!"

"Jeff stunk," said Jordan.

"He killed us with penalties!" said Stuart, shaking his head.

Tom grimaced. "He missed my perfect goal!"

"Some *friend*!" they agreed.

"Let's check out our team stats on the computer," Tom said. His friends left their boots at the door and followed him to his mom's office. He clicked on the Internet symbol and scrolled down to the website for Hockey Calgary. "Here we are!" The boys huddled around the screen.

"We're tied for second!" said Stuart. "What happened? We were first!"

"Who are we tied with?" asked Jordan.

"Um . . ." Tom followed the chart. "The Bears."

"See?" snapped Mark. "We should have won that game and we'd still be first! The Bears were behind us!"

Tom's mom called from the kitchen, "While you're on the computer, Tom, please send Jeff a reminder about babysitting on Monday."

Tom pulled up his mom's e-mail program and found Jeff's address.

"Wow!" said Jordan. "You're good at this."

"Let me see," said Stuart.

Tom started the message.

Dear Jeff,

With a funny smile on his face, he typed:

**We were robbed! My goal
should have counted.**

Mark laughed. "Yeah. ROBBED! It was a
stickup. Get it? A hockey stick up! Hey, let
me write some." He pushed Tom away from
the keyboard.

**I didn't really high stick. And
mouthguards make me gag.
And they could give you
buckteeth.**

Everyone snickered.

"No more penalties! No more penalties!"
they chanted.

Then Jordan added:

**You stink. Sorry. We don't like
stinkers.**

Stuart finished off with:

**From the guys you used to be
nice to:**

Tom, Stuart, Jordan and Mark

He inserted four unhappy faces:

☹ ☹ ☹ ☹

They were all laughing. Tom read the whole e-mail as his friends chanted, "No more penalties! No more penalties! Jeff is the worst! Jeff is the worst!" over and over.

A cool shiver went up Tom's back. "Whoa, whoa!" he said. "We gotta delete this and e-mail him about the babysitting. Besides, we don't hate *him* — we just hate some of the *rules*. That picky I-can't-see-the-puck rule cost us the game."

Tom moved the mouse to delete the message. He clicked. "Oh, no!" he gasped. "I think I screwed up."

The screen said, *Sending*. A picture of an envelope flew across the bottom of the e-mail.

Everyone spoke at the same time. "I was joking." "What happened?" "We didn't mean it." "Why did your mom tell us to e-mail anyway?"

"Quick!" Tom panicked. "We have to send him another one." He wrote:

Please please please ignore the last e-mail. It was a bad bad joke.

He pressed the Send symbol again. He stared at the blank computer screen and then at his friends. They all looked guilty. Tom felt horrible. His stomach spun the way it did at hockey tryouts. "Do you think the first e-mail really went to Jeff?"

"We don't have e-mail, so I don't know," said Jordan.

"Jeff can take a joke, right?" asked Mark.

"We were just kidding," added Stuart.

Tom sighed. "What should we do now?"

"I gotta get home," said Jordan.

The others nodded.

"Hey, Hawks — we're dead ducks," mumbled Mark, jamming on his boots.

— ● —

Tom felt sick. He crawled into bed, zapped. His thoughts were jumbled up like a wad of old hockey tape covered in sock lint. He was mad Mark hadn't worn his mouthguard. He was glad the Bear got a penalty for tripping him. He was glad the Bears' first goal was called off. He was mad his own goal was called off. He wished he'd asked Coach Howie to explain offside again. He wished he hadn't pressed Send by mistake.

Tom thought about Jeff. *Why did I tell him we were robbed? Why did Jordan say he stunk?*

Jeff usually babysat Monday. And that was tomorrow.

Tom began to sweat.

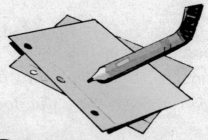

Classroom Rules

Monday afternoon after recess.

Mrs. Wong stood beside the "Our City" bulletin board, looking at the drawings. "Wonderful. Wonderful. We have a firefighter . . . the Flames goalie . . . a nurse . . . Officer Woz . . . a Zamboni operator . . . a carpenter . . . a hairdresser . . . a referee . . ."

Tom looked at the nice picture he had drawn of Jeff. The stripes went straight up and down. He wore a big smile. Tom wondered if Jeff was smiling today.

"Now for the final copies of your questions," said Mrs. Wong. "Let's see.

Jordan has a question beside his Flames goalie picture." She read: "How can hockey help our city?" Mrs. Wong smiled. "Good question, Jordan." She scrunched up her forehead. "I want to answer this one! I think hockey gives Calgary more city spirit. I own a Flames jersey and I have a flag on my car!"

"Go, Flames, go!" cheered some of the kids.

Mrs. Wong is right, thought Tom. *Hockey spirit is fun.* But he didn't feel the spirit right now. Right now he felt pukey.

"Oh, my!" exclaimed Mrs. Wong, looking at the biggest picture on the bulletin board. "That looks like me!"

Kylie said, "It *is*! With diamond earrings! Read my first question, Mrs. Wong."

"Okay, it's: How do you decide what rules to make for the class?" Mrs. Wong thought for a moment. "Well, my rules are all about safety, respect and schoolwork. I always try to be fair. Rules make things fair for everyone." She clapped and sang out, "I stay cool with classroom rules!"

Tom smiled. He liked Mrs. Wong.

She looked at her watch. "Okay, people, *if* you have your questions on our bulletin board, and *if* you've read the Monopoly rules, you can play Monopoly till the bell rings."

"Amber! Jill!" said Kylie. "C'mon, let's take the purple table!"

"Woo-eee, Monopoly!" Everyone headed for the games. Everyone except Tom. He looked at his blank page and let out a big sigh. He knew it was fair. Mrs. Wong was just enforcing her finish-your-homework-first rule.

Tom sat at his desk listening to the other kids play Monopoly.

"I'm buying Boardwalk." "I got Free Parking!" "Roll the dice." "Go directly to Jail." "That'll be 50 bucks." "Your turn."

He tried to think up some good city helper questions for his picture of Jeff. *Should they be about babysitting? Or should they be about reffing?* His mind was frozen on one thing — the e-mail.

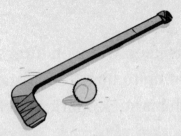

Winning Isn't Everything

At four o'clock, the boys were at Tom's house, playing road hockey. Stuart and Mark were teamed against Tom, trying to score on Jordan. The score was 3–0 for Stuart and Mark.

Stuart had the ball. He quickly passed to Mark. Mark unleashed a hard slapshot. *Bam!* The ball flew into the net.

"Yes!" raved Stuart. "We got another one!"

Tom needed help, playing against two. Where was Jeff?

Jordan tossed the ball down the street.

Tom sprinted after it. *Go, go, go,* he told

himself. His feet were on fire. Stuart and Mark caught up to him. Tom turned, hugging the ball with his stick. Mark snatched it away — again.

Tom sighed, frustrated. Two against one was a rip-off. How could he win? He didn't have a chance.

Mark passed the ball to Stuart. Stuart easily passed it back to Mark. Suddenly Tom

jabbed just a bit of his stick between Mark's legs.

"*Aaiii!*" shrieked Mark. He wiped out.

Tom got hold of the ball and fired a blazing shot. *SMACK!* It hit the crossbar, sliding the net across the pavement. Jordan centred the net while Stuart ran down the street, chasing the loose, bouncing ball.

Mark picked himself up and brushed off the snow. His jeans had a big hole at the knee.

Tom banged his stick. "No goal, again!"

Mark pointed at him. "Hey, you tripped me! That's a dirty move — just because you want to score!"

"Me, dirty? You get more penalties than anyone on the team!" blurted Tom. "Remember, the Bears scored when *you* had a penalty!"

Mark glared.

"Come on, guys! Quit fighting!" said

Stuart. "Winning isn't everything!"

Tom looked at Mark's ripped knee. And tripping wasn't fair. "Sorry."

"Okay, let's go!" Stuart shot the ball back into play to Mark. When Mark turned, Tom was there. He lifted the ball off Mark's stick and ran with it. Jordan crouched in net. Tom circled wide, then flicked the ball back. It flew into the net.

"Goal!" cheered Tom, pumping his fist in the air. "Finally!"

"What a shot!" said Jordan.

"Awesome!" howled Stuart.

"Yeah," said Mark, punching Tom's shoulder. "You rule!"

Stuart held his fist out and the boys banged their fists on top. "Road rats!"

Tom looked down the street. Where was Jeff?

Time Out

A car was slowly creeping toward them.

"Hey, it's my Grandma Dot!" Tom waved. *What is she doing here?* he wondered.

Grandma Dot parked her car and got out, holding a large cookie tin. "Hello, boys," she said. "How about a time out?" She took off the lid and each of them happily gobbled down a soft cookie loaded with chocolate chips. "That was some hockey game you boys played the other day."

Jordan growled, "We lost."

"I saw that," said Grandma Dot.

"We were really mad," said Tom. "We got all these penalties called on us."

"Well, I got one too — a parking ticket. Rules are rules! Now, come on in, Tom. It's too cold to be playing on the street. And it's dangerous!"

Jordan nudged Stuart. Stuart nudged Mark. When Jeff babysat, they always played on the street, even when it was snowing.

Tom whispered to his friends, "Come back after dinner. We'll play road hockey, eat more cookies and maybe Jeff will be here."

Grandma Dot said, "After dinner, Tom has a few things to do — including homework, I'm sure." She smiled.

"What about Jeff?" asked Stuart.

Grandma Dot picked up the ball and put it in her bag. "I'm the babysitter." She walked toward the house and opened the front door. "Say goodbye to your friends, Tom."

But what about Jeff? Tom's stomach flipped.

"Do you think he quit?" asked Jordan.

"Inside, right now!" hollered Grandma Dot.

Jeff quit? Tom felt like he'd been bodychecked. He wanted to cry — just like he did the time he was bodychecked into the boards.

Shared Respect

Tom put his hockey gloves and boots in the mudroom. A puck-sized lump was stuck in his throat.

"What first — a shower or your homework?" asked Grandma Dot.

"Well-l-l-l . . ." said Tom, "part of my homework is Monopoly . . ."

"Wonderful!" said Grandma Dot. They set up the board. "How about I let you have two turns to my one," she offered. "And you can skip going to Jail. And you can collect *five* hundred dollars when you pass Go!"

"Grandma!" said Tom. "It'll be too easy!"

"Don't you like to win?" She winked.

Tom thought about it. *I do love winning. It always feels better than losing. But — had she* let *me win? All those times?* A little light bulb went on in his brain. "You mean I'm *not* the best Monopoly player?" He looked right into Grandma Dot's eyes.

"Well, maybe I gave you just a bit of an advantage once or twice," she admitted.

"Oh, boy. Oh, man. Well, no more!" said Tom. "I have to play by the rules. *All* the rules. Because next week I might get to play Officer Woz. And it's got to be a fair game!"

Grandma Dot smiled. "Okay, Tom, you asked for it! No more half-price properties!" She handed Tom the Monopoly rules.

Tom began to read.

"From now on, look out," said Grandma Dot, "because I'm really good at this game. And I'm going to be a stickler for the rules."

"You're on!" said Tom. He wondered if he

would ever beat her at Monopoly again. *Gee, it's kind of fun to think I'll have to try my best, play by all the rules and not be so sure I'll win.*

Then Grandma Dot's cellphone rang and she went to the hall to talk.

Tom had an idea. *I could work on my other homework.* He grabbed his backpack and sat at the kitchen table. He tapped his hockey pencil, thinking about questions and Jeff. Finally, he wrote:

Dear Jeff,

It's not good to tell a ref he stinks.

"Nope!" Tom scrunched up the paper. He started again.

Dear Jeff,

It's good for a ref to be a stickler.

Get it? Hockey stick — stickler.

"Nope!" Tom scrunched up the paper. He started again.

Dear Jeff,

Sorry again about the e-mail. Will you please be my babysitter? We like you very very very much.

Tom pressed so hard on his pencil that it snapped in half. He looked for some tape in the drawer. When he couldn't find any, he went to his hockey bag for his sock tape. It was stuck to Jeff's little book, *Hockey Canada: Official Playing Rules.*

On the cover, there was a picture of a ref and a message. It said: "Shared Respect. Players. Coaches. Officials. Parents." Tom opened it. On page twelve, there was a message from Hockey Canada: "A game should be refereed strictly in accordance with the rules."

Every rule was there in black and white — with pictures. Every rule was clearly spelled out by Hockey Canada — every rule the Hawks had broken. Jeff was only trying to be the best ref.

Tom wrapped a piece of sock tape around his pencil. He held onto the wiggly part and wrote,

Being a ref must be hard. You have to skate really fast. And know when to blow your whistle. You have to remember all the rules — even the ones nobody likes. Mrs. Wong said a teacher makes rules to be fair. You showed me that a ref has to follow the hockey rules, no matter what.

Too bad if his friends don't like it.

From your friend, Tom

PS: Winning isn't everything.

PPS: You can eat all the cookies.

PPPS: You don't really stink.

PPPS: Please STICK with me. Get it?

Hockey stick!

At the bottom, Tom drew a ref jersey with his black marker. Then he folded the letter and put it in Grandma Dot's cookie tin. Maybe she

would drive him to Jeff's house if he asked. He could leave the tin on Jeff's steps.

Tom sighed. He wished he'd stopped himself and his friends from writing the bad stuff. He closed his eyes and imagined a giant ref's whistle. *WHEEEEE!* STOP! Suddenly, Tom thought of a great question for Jeff for the class project: *How would hockey games be different if there weren't any rules?*

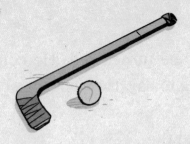

Hockey Rules!

Grandma Dot came into the kitchen.

"Oh dear," she said, looking out the window and buttoning her coat. "It's snowing." She patted Tom on the shoulder. "I'd better get home before the roads get bad."

"You're leaving?" said Tom.

"Jeff's here now. He'll babysit till your mom and dad get home," said Grandma Dot, opening the door. "I was only a *call-up* till he got here." She waved goodbye. "See you at your game. Go, Hawks, go!"

Jeff stepped inside. His hair was wet and his cheeks were glowing red.

Tom's face turned red. He couldn't think of anything to say. He went to get the cookie tin.

Jeff read the letter a couple of times. He ate a couple of cookies.

Tom gulped back a sick feeling. *What is he thinking?* he wondered.

Finally, Jeff said, "I've been playing hockey for years. I didn't always like the refs' calls either. I got suspended three times. Once I broke my arm. Then I figured it out. When I played my best — *and* played by the rules — there was nothing better." Jeff stuffed another cookie into his mouth. "And now I know how hard it is to be a ref."

Tom breathed a sigh of relief. *Phew.* Jeff

wasn't too mad after all. He was so cool.

"Maybe one day you'll be a ref and you'll find out!" Jeff ruffled Tom's hair.

Tom smiled. He'd like to be a ref one day. He was glad he'd chosen Jeff the Ref for the city project.

Jeff reached into his duffle bag. He pulled out a bag of four green blobby things. "Mouthguards. They were giving them away free at the refs' clinic," he said. "Give one to Mark, okay? You know you guys gotta wear them to prevent injuries. And penalties!" He winked.

"Thanks!" Tom smiled. "Can I phone him and tell him?"

"Sure!" Jeff smiled back. "Invite him over. And Stuart and Jordan. Let's play road hockey!" He downed two more cookies.

"Woo hoo!" yelped Tom. "And we're playing full rules now." He grabbed his Flames jersey and pulled it over his head.

"You're on!" Jeff opened the front door. Snow fluttered down in the light from the street lamp. As they got the net from the garage, Tom asked, "Do you think, if you got invited, you'd be able to visit my classroom?"

———— ● ————

When Stuart, Mark and Jordan arrived, they approached Jeff shyly.

Stuart spoke for them. "We're sorry for the e-mail." All three faces were serious.

"Here. These are for you." Mark held out a bag of pickle chips. "I'm really going to watch raising my stick."

Jeff flashed his crooked smile. "Hockey rules! Shared respect!"

As Jordan buckled his goalie pads, Jeff said, "Okay, men — Tom says it's full rules from now on, so I have to teach you one more . . ." His face turned mischievous. "When the Flames are in the playoffs — NO shaving! It's bad luck!"

Everyone cracked up.

Tom reached into his pocket and pulled out his black marker. He scribbled a crooked line above his upper lip. "Who else wants a moustache?"

"Me! Me!" said Mark. "A big droopy one!"

"Give me a beard," said Stuart.

"Beard and moustache for me," snorted Jordan.

"Goatee, right here," said Jeff, pointing to his chin.

When they were done they looked at each

other and fell back on the snowbank, laughing.

Jeff held up the road hockey ball. "Okay road-rat dudes, I'm ready! It's hockey time!"

He dropped the ball and passed it to Tom.

Tom took a shot. "Yahoo!" he shouted. "Game on!"

Jeff really is the best sitter in the world, he thought. *And the best ref.*